THE RANGER OBJECTIVE

AN AMERICAN MERCENARY SHORT STORY

JASON KASPER

D1602239

Severn River

Severn River Publishing
www.SevernRiverPublishing.com

ISBN: 978-1-951249-47-2 (Paperback)

For information contact:

Jason@Jason-Kasper.com

Jason-Kasper.com

Be the first to learn about new releases and get free newsletter only
bonus content by signing up at jason-kasper.com/newsletter

To all the vets that brought their battles home.

THE RANGER OBJECTIVE

September 11, 2002
Shigal Valley
Kunar Province, Afghanistan

The machinegun grip felt cool and reassuring in my hand as I maneuvered the barrel from my rocky vantage point.

While the valley floor far below me swarmed with emerald treetops, the windswept Afghan mountainsides rising from either side of it comprised the most unforgiving terrain I could imagine. Impossibly steep hills were terraced with primitive clusters of buildings that appeared to be carved out of the mountain, and the remaining rock faces were sliced by thin plateaus teeming with crops.

My machinegun sights stopped at a small cluster of mud buildings with flat roofs, their surfaces an identical shade of tan to the stony hillsides around them. How could people occupy such a rugged and alien landscape? Yet I caught glimpses of colorful clothing slipping between buildings as people went about their chores, and the sound of bleating goats and barking dogs reached me between erratic bursts of mountain wind.

There was not a scrap of visible human progress that exceeded the Stone Age. Nestled just across the border from the tribal region of northwest Pakistan, these people truly existed in a forgotten corner of the earth. The greatest infusion of technology in this entire valley was automatic weapons and rockets made in distant lands— some belonging to us, and some to the enemy.

Glancing down the hill to my left, I saw the Ranger squad filing down a rocky cliff face toward the buildings. The soldiers appeared as small tan figures maneuvering into position with an assortment of dark weapons. It was a moving sight: Rangers sweeping up the valley wearing American flags on the first anniversary of the September 11 attacks.

Just one year earlier, I'd been nearing the end of Basic Training, a journey that had—

"All right, Slick." I heard Remy's Alabamian drawl beside me. "Pop off that gun."

He slid a can of dip back into the shoulder pocket of his desert fatigues, spitting the first long stream of wintergreen tobacco juice onto the ground beside him.

"Listen, Remy," I began, fondly stroking the grip, "me and this machinegun were made for each other. Sometimes you just know. How else could it feel so...so *right*?"

"Well, when I get killed you can carry that sumbitch all day. Till then, you're still my AG. Pop off."

I pushed myself left and he slid his lanky frame behind the machinegun, settling into place with a practiced repetition. One hand was against the buttstock, cheek resting on knuckles as he rocked the massive weapon forward on its bipod and scanned for movement below.

Of course he looked natural, I thought. Remy had been in the unit for two years, and, at legal drinking age, was practically a senior citizen among our group of privates.

I settled onto the rock surface beside him with considerably less finesse, adjusting the heavy belt of machinegun ammo stretching from my rucksack to the gun. Then I picked up my assault rifle and joined Remy in scanning the village, though that was secondary in my job as the AG.

The assistant gunner.

The new guy.

Carry the ammo, and let Remy do the shooting.

Sure, I was supposed to spot targets for him as well, but an experienced gunner like Remy didn't need my help any more than a pro quarterback needed a water boy.

Scanning through my rifle optic, I asked, "So where are all these barrel-chested Islamic fighters we're supposed to be schwacking right now?" I swept my sights across the distant slits of shadow beneath roof overhangs. If someone was going to contest the arrival of a Ranger squad searching for weapon caches, I thought, that's where they'd emerge.

Hearing no immediate response from Remy, I added, "Shigal Valley is supposed to be so badass, I thought we'd be knee-deep in Taliban bodies by now."

Finally Remy replied, "First mission of the trip. They can't all be winners, Slick. Have some patience."

"Easy for you to say. I was stuck in the asbestos-death-trap barracks at Airborne School last year while you were parachuting into Afghanistan, racking up confirmed kills and delivering American justice at six hundred rounds per minute. How many bad guys did you tag that first night?"

He shook his head slightly behind the machinegun

sights. "Slick, you probably know better than I do after making me tell you the story so many damn times."

"I didn't 'make' you, Remy. You were *obligated* to tell me once for every three times you asked to see a picture of my girlfriend. It's called a barter system."

"Well," he offered, "you won't need to hear about the last deployment for much longer. You're gonna have your own stories soon enough."

"That's what I thought, too, until my first couple days on patrol have been dry hole after dry hole."

"What do you expect, Slick? This entire valley's got a bunch of Rangers up its ass right now. With machineguns, rockets, attack helicopters—"

"Helicopters are refueling," I corrected him. "So why isn't anyone shooting at us yet?"

He released a mighty sigh. "When I was as cherry as you are, I used to pray to the god of war too. But remember, this shit ain't no fun when the rabbit's got the gun."

"Oh, it'll be fun. We're on a Ranger patrol in Afghanistan on the first anniversary of 9/11." Smiling, I reached back and patted a pouch holding my rolled American flag. "This couldn't be any more patriotic if we wrapped ourselves in our flags."

Remy paused for a long time after that.

Then he said, "Know why every Ranger carries an American flag, Slick? It ain't patriotism. If you get killed, that's what we cover your body with till the MEDEVAC comes."

Our radios crackled to life before I could reply.

"*Gun Six,*" the squad leader transmitted, "*we're preparing to make entry on the outbuildings.*"

Remy didn't move, eyes fixed behind the machinegun. "Tell 'em we got nuthin' and we're ready."

I looked up from my rifle optic and touched my radio

without keying the button to transmit. Then I said in Remy's Southern accent, "We got nuthin' and we're ready."

"Shit ain't funny!" Remy scolded.

"How does that not get old?" I asked no one in particular, then keyed my radio to transmit, "Gun Six copies, no movement to report. Standing by for visual."

The Ranger squad below had vanished from view behind a cluster of trees. I gave a final scan of the objective, half expecting to see Afghan men fleeing or preparing to ambush any approaching American soldiers.

But the village was now deathly still.

A Ranger point man stepped out from the tree line, leading his fire team toward the outbuildings while the other half of the squad remained stationary to cover their movement.

"Gebhart's in the open," I said to Remy.

"I see him. Shifting right. Make sure that—"

I heard the blast of a sniper rifle, and Gebhart fell in place before the shot's echo swept over the hills.

The response from the Ranger squad was immediate as they returned fire, the chattering bursts from their automatic weapons spilling across the valley. Clouds of red fog blossomed around Gebhart's body as smoke grenades provided concealment for his recovery. Someone in the squad fired a rocket that streaked upward, slicing through the sky before exploding on the hill to our right.

"Pack up!" Remy shouted. I unsnapped the links binding my ammo belt to the machinegun as the squad leader's voice came over the radio.

"Gun Six, get on top of that ridge to your right. You're going to see a dark patch of woods on the hilltop. Burn it the fuck down, that's where the sniper is hiding—"

Remy was already pushing himself upright, lifting the machinegun and running toward the high ground by the time I slipped my arms through my rucksack straps. Struggling to my feet like an upended turtle against the anvil of machinegun ammo now anchored to my back, I almost left my assault rifle behind before snatching it as an afterthought.

Turning amid the reverberating howl of the firefight between the Ranger squad and an enemy sniper, I caught sight of Remy's gangly figure hauling the machinegun uphill. I raced after him, fighting for breath in the thin mountain air, the inside of my mouth coated with a film of sand.

The surreally high-pitched chirp of Ranger grenade launchers punched through the air, countered by the resulting crash of their high explosive rounds beyond the ridge I now approached.

Remy's voice over my radio: "—*shift fire left, Gun Six on high ground*—"

The low *crump* of another impacting grenade round echoed against the cacophony of automatic weapons, interspersed with the jangle of the exposed ammo belt slapping against my rucksack. I could feel the long, snaking chain of machinegun ammo shifting on my back, disrupting my forward momentum as Remy's form disappeared over the crest.

He was on his own. I couldn't keep up, and yet I couldn't possibly move any faster.

I reached the bottom of the slope and launched myself into a frantic uphill scramble. An ornate stone formation guarded the crest of the hill, and I desperately fought against gravity to reach it.

As I battled up the sandy, rock-strewn hillside, I heard the squad leader's voice on my radio: "—*confirm shift fire, lay waste up there, Remy*—"

Pulling myself atop the ridge at last, I saw sloping

terrain dotted with scrub brush and low trees. A long stretch of exposed rock gave way to a darkly forested patch of woods: the sniper's hiding spot, exactly as the squad leader had described.

And it was being decimated by the Ranger squad.

Brown clouds rose between shadowy pine trees as the puffs of impacting bullets and grenade rounds felled boughs, which crashed to the earth as Ranger counterfire chopped the forest apart.

Yet the sound of another sniper shot sliced through the din.

"—fuck over here now, David!"

Remy's voice jarred me out of my daze of disbelief, and I followed the sound to find him already in the prone position, gun pointing at the woods from a shallow depression in the dirt.

Racing to his left, I spun and fell backwards, letting my rucksack absorb the impact. I writhed out of the straps, then rolled onto my belly and yanked the ammo belt free.

Remy seamlessly held his firing position as I struggled to manipulate the dull gray metal links to connect my ammo belt with the short string of rounds still hanging from the machinegun. My hands were slippery with sweat, the bullet casings sliding out of place beneath my fingertips.

"Come on, Slick!"

Finally I managed to hook an empty C-shaped link around the first bullet casing in Remy's ammo belt, feeling the *snap* that connected my rucksack full of ammo to the gun.

I shouted, "We're linked!"

Those two words had barely left my mouth before Remy thumbed the safety off his machinegun and opened fire.

The sky around us thudded with the rapid booming cadence of the machinegun roaring to life. It chomped through the belt of ammo that I now pulled from my rucksack in increments, the massive gun ravenous for the hundreds of linked bullets waiting to be launched into a forest that hid an unseen sniper.

Beneath the frenetic pace of machinegun bursts was the thin clatter of brass and links piling up on the rock surface below as the mountain air became choked by gunpowder.

The humming cackle of machinegun fire was soothing, reassuring in its calibrated familiarity, bringing order to chaos. Remy's gun was the most casualty-producing weapon in an entire Ranger platoon, much less the single squad below, and I felt myself grinning as he brought it into the fight, raking a stream of fire-orange tracer rounds across the swath of dark woods.

Another sniper shot rang out.

"*Gun Six*," the squad leader transmitted breathlessly, "*be advised, we're still taking effective sniper fire.*"

I looked to Remy for guidance on my response and instead saw him break his grip on the machinegun to key his own radio.

"Roger, we can try and maneuver closer."

"*Negative, stay in place. We recovered Gebhart, he's gonna make it. Apaches are inbound for airstrike before the MEDEVAC chopper lands. ETA less than ten mikes.*"

"Copy, Gun Six remaining in place." I felt a rush of elation upon hearing that Gebhart hadn't been killed, but after releasing his radio, Remy spat to the side and hissed "*Fuck*" before resuming his grip on the buttstock without firing.

"What?" I picked up my assault rifle and scanned the darkly wooded hilltop for movement.

"Nuthin'. We'll just have to get that sniper another day."

"What do you mean, another day? Apaches are about to turn those woods into a dumpster fire." I looked around the hilltop. "He's got nowhere to go except toward Rangers or on a death fall down the mountain."

"He knows that. Bet you a paycheck there's a way out on the other side of this hill."

"What are you, the Taliban Whisperer? How can you know?"

Remy spat again, and when he spoke next he sounded disgusted. "We're fighting human beings now, not hunting white-tailed deer. This sniper's no amateur, Slick. He didn't hit us until our birds were off-station. He knows our tactics as well as we do. Soon as he hears rotor blades headed his way, he's gone."

"We've got two more days on this patrol," I panted in disbelief, still trying to catch my breath. "If he gets away he's going to shoot another Ranger before we leave the valley." Looking to Remy, I concluded, "Unless you want to see one of our boys covered by his own American flag, we need to kill this sniper while he's still in front of us."

"'Course we do. The catch is gettin' that done without being the next casualties. That's why he's got us dead to rights."

"We can relocate around the hill, find his escape route. When he runs, we drill him. Mission complete."

Remy sounded composed now, resigning himself to the situation. "Negative, Slick. We're staying put until those Apaches get here and light up the hilltop. We take this machinegun near the woods, that sniper will hear us coming and smoke us both. You're crawfishin' between a *possible* Ranger casualty in the next two days versus two *guaranteed* casualties right now: you and me."

He was right. Both the machinegun and its ammo were loud and exceedingly cumbersome to move. The two of us would give ourselves away long before we got close enough to make a difference.

Then my mind's eye replayed the scene of Gebhart falling in place, victim to the sniper's bullet. But when the body hit the ground, splayed out in a pool of blood, it was no longer Gebhart in my imagination.

It was Remy.

Shaking the thought clear, I glanced sideways to see my gunner alive and well beside me, his slight jawline bulging with a wad of dip.

I lifted my cheek from the stock of the assault rifle and gazed into the dark, distant forest. Looking sideways, then behind me, and then past Remy, I considered the terrain, assessing the low ground and blind spots around us. A breeze blew overhead, chilling the sweat-soaked fatigues clinging to my back. The acrid gun smoke grew stale before losing itself in the wind.

Swallowing hard, I opened a pocket in my rucksack and withdrew a single smoke grenade, then slid the metal canister into a cargo pocket of my fatigue pants. "Remy, you need to keep shooting."

"Naw, Slick. We'd be wasting ammo now. I can't kill the sniper—"

"Not to kill the sniper," I panted, feeling my chest constrict even as I spoke with dead certainty. "To cover the sound."

"Sound of *what?*"

I drew a final breath, then grabbed my radio and spoke into it. "Cease fire on forest, David maneuvering on enemy sniper. Remy will provide covering fire."

Remy looked at me with an expression somewhere between shock and disbelief. "I told you that shit ain't funny. I know you didn't transmit. Didn't even do your bull-sheeyit accent."

The squad leader replied, "*Negative, negative—*"

Grabbing my assault rifle and rolling away from Remy, I pushed myself to my feet and began to run. Remy's hand swiped my boot as he tried to grab me, but I wrenched away and sped down the hill behind him.

As I circled around the hilltop in a flanking maneuver, staying in the low ground and out of view from the dark forest, I half expected Remy to tackle me from behind.

Instead, I heard him open fire with the machinegun.

I'd left Remy no choice—he either had to abandon his gun and try to catch me or continue shooting in begrudging support of my plan. He'd chosen the latter.

Between his machinegun bursts, I caught him transmitting to the line squad.

"*David's maneuvering, cease fire...*"

I was running as I never had before, rounding the low ground beside the forest. No machinegun ammo, no rucksack weighing me down; instead I was free to choose, free to react instinctively.

Glancing down the hill to my right, I took in the surroundings as if looking to them for reassurance. Blotches of darkness pooled beneath scattered trees on the hills around me, rising out of the dead earth. The bottom of the mountain was swathed in a belt of shadow, its natural beauty concealed by the absence of light.

The valley beneath me slid away into sharply mottled creases, while my immediate terrain deteriorated the farther I proceeded along my flanking maneuver. Crumbling rocks littered the hillside, and errant scrub brush was the only vegetation in sight. No cover, no concealment. And while I was well out of the sniper's view from the hilltop forest, I was also far beyond sight of any

Ranger forces. I'd have to keep moving, find the escape route before setting up a hasty ambush for the sniper that would soon flee.

As I cut left around the far side of the hilltop, I grabbed at rock crevices packed with vines and gnarled tree roots. Emerging from the low ground and heading toward the hilltop, I glanced beyond a layer of stone outcroppings to make out glimpses of the darkened treetops.

The sharp slope was now so steep that I had to rotate my rifle to my back and scramble up on all fours. Loose earth and stray rocks scattered downward beneath me, but Remy's comforting machinegun bursts concealed my noise.

I began to make out patches of light blue sky through the treetops, but as I reached the hilltop ledge, the view was soon obscured by the forest's edges. My heart was hammering in my chest, my ears ringing from the earlier gunfire, my brow oozing sweat that ran in rivulets down the side of my face.

I slid around a tangle of dry scrub brush too thick to push my way through and stopped beside a tree trunk to scan for the sniper's escape route.

To my relief, the route was there, just as Remy said it would be. The lone path out of the dark forest was a thin strip of woods that bridged the saddle leading to the next hilltop. Any other direction out of the forest led either toward Rangers or into a sheer rock face too steep to negotiate on foot.

I tasted metal and smelled clouds of dust from the Ranger counterfire that had ended minutes ago. Now that I had a clear view of the escape route, I carefully slid into a kneeling firing position and readied my weapon in anticipation of the sniper's appearance.

My radio projected Remy's garbled voice.

"*...need to check in, Slick...*"

A sharp *crack* from a sniper round split the tree trunk beside me. I flung myself downward as the gunshot echoed in my skull, the loudest noise I'd ever heard. Between panting breaths, I caught a whiff of burning pine from the bullet smoldering in the tree next to my head.

I glanced up and saw the scrub brush around me, traces of sunlight glinting off delicate branches that trembled in the wind.

Why wasn't I scared?

A second round split the air over my head, followed by a third that churned a divot of earth a few feet to my left.

I slid backward down the rock face and out of sight from the woods, keying my radio.

"I made it to the other side," I exhaled. "I have his escape route covered."

Remy sounded furious. "*You ain't got shit covered! Apaches are a few minutes out and ground-to-air comms are down. They can't reach the pilots to call off the strike. Get your ass back here!*"

I looked to both sides, considering my options. While the sniper knew my current location, I could still move even closer to the wooded saddle between hills, my only chance of repositioning myself while still cutting off his escape route.

To move in any other direction, including back toward Remy, would be to save the sniper's life. Two days left on our patrol, and zero chance he wouldn't take another shot at us.

Thumbing the transmit button on my radio, I said, "I'll get the sniper first. Going off comms."

"*No, goddamnit, those Apaches will—*"

I turned off the radio, then scrambled downhill and

cut across the low ground to move even further from Remy, closing the distance between me and the sniper's only way out.

My pulse was racing, heart slamming as I reached the strip of vegetation dipping into a faraway hill. I took up a covered position behind a tree that gave me a vantage point both ways. The dark patch of woods loomed on the hilltop, dangerously close and impenetrably dense. Placing my assault rifle stock against my shoulder, I waited to see what the sniper's next move would be with a single thought.

Checkmate, motherfucker.

But my elation came too soon, and when the sniper cast his vote on how the gunfight would proceed, it almost killed me outright.

His next shot whizzed so close to my head that a loud ringing erupted in my left ear.

I didn't take cover and valorously return fire as my training dictated; instead, an animalistic instinct caused me to fling myself backward, landing hard before crawling behind another tree as more bullets snapped through the air around me.

The sniper was trying to finish me off from afar, I realized, before he sprinted across the saddle to freedom. He knew he couldn't move any nearer until I was dead. His sniper rifle was virtually useless at close range, whereas my assault rifle would dominate a battle of reflexive fire. His safety was in distance, mine in proximity.

If I remained stationary, he'd locate a firing position in the dark woods from which to finish me off for good—we both knew the Apaches were on their way to annihilate us. Either one of us would emerge alive, or neither of us would. No other options were possible.

I either had to turn the tables right now or end up being covered with my American flag.

A replay of Remy's voice echoed in my mind: *This sniper's no amateur, Slick...He knows our tactics as well as we do.*

My only chance of killing the sniper, I knew at once, was to violate all military tactics.

I slid the smoke grenade from my cargo pocket, pulling the ring and flinging it to my right as hard as I could. A hollow *pop* preceded the zinging hiss of the grenade coming to life, and seconds later I could see a billowing fog of crimson rising up among the trees.

The sniper opened fire, shooting rounds into the smoke. With his precision scope, he could only focus on one thing at a time—and if he was trying to hit someone using the smoke to conceal their movement, then he wasn't watching the exposed ground in the opposite direction. I jumped to my feet and sprinted left, away from the smoke.

And mere moments before the sniper realized his mistake, I plunged into the forest.

My ploy had bought me only seconds, but they were seconds I desperately needed to close the gap. By the time the sniper caught my movement in his peripheral vision, I was inside the grove of trees concealing him. He reoriented his rifle toward me, betraying a shift of movement in the underbrush—and I sped toward it via a circuitous route to keep as many trees between us as I could.

The next fifteen seconds were a zigzagging sprint of feverish intensity as I darted from cover to cover in the thickly wooded tangle of trees and brush. My vision registered green moss smeared across the stones below me and blurry images of pine boughs to my front. Then I caught sight of a spark of flame from his muzzle blast as rounds cracked through the air, bullets slicing into tree trunks and snapping through branches as I ran.

But the closer I got, the less accurate his fire grew. His shots became a beating snare drum until they abruptly stopped altogether—he was reloading.

Now within ten feet, it was my turn to send the sniper for cover. I fired half a dozen rounds toward him as he scrambled away. Then I broke into an all-out sprint, vaulting a fallen tree toward a head-on impasse with my enemy. Facing the greatest pressure I'd ever experienced, my focus was steeled to the single task in front of me. There would be no second chances.

I took a sharp sidestep right as I approached the location of the muzzle flash. Seeing another blur of movement amid the brush, I fired three more rounds at it while still moving at a full run.

Bang bang bang.

The sound of my shots ended in a human cry.

Skidding to a stop, I pivoted in place and took aim toward the noise. I fired twice more. A man rolled sideways on the ground, dropping the rifle magazine he'd been trying to reload. I centered my aim on his torso, finger tensing against the trigger. Then I froze in place, horrified.

My mind couldn't process what I was seeing—had I just shot an American?

He was no Afghan fighter, but a man as white as I was, with short-cropped hair and a bushy red beard. He was wincing in pain and disbelief. Was he from some Special Forces recon team I didn't know about?

But the sniper rifle beside him was a Soviet Dragunov.

One side of his mottled camouflage jacket was darkened with a slick of bright red, as if he'd fallen in a puddle of scarlet paint. His eyes met mine, unapologetic. With my weapon at the ready, I stared into icy blue irises that smoldered as life slipped from them.

"*Chyort voz'mi...*" he gasped, in what sounded like Russian. "*Ty zhe prosto pacan.*"

He wasn't American or Afghan, I realized, but a foreign fighter from Chechnya.

At first I couldn't believe it—after circling the globe with my comrades in pursuit of Taliban or Al Qaeda, I'd instead come face-to-face with a Caucasian man who'd traveled from an Islamic Russian republic to wage jihad against the Americans.

I didn't consciously fire my next rounds. Instead, I simply felt the rifle tensing against my shoulder as if of its own accord, followed by the sound of blasting shots until those blue eyes went vacant.

Then I reloaded, stuffing the partially spent rifle magazine in my cargo pocket, the action reflexive after hundreds of repetitions in training. Viewed from a distance, I would have appeared a consummate warrior: fearless, robotic in my lethality.

But in my mind, the situation was far different—I was a nineteen-year-old kid standing on an unnamed hilltop on the far side of the world, my first encounter with an enemy combatant now a corpse who looked like any number of men in my Virginia hometown, which now seemed a lifetime away.

My thoughts were foggy, dreamlike, but my actions were automated: crisp and precise and in stark contrast to the awkward fumbling of the Ranger private and assistant gunner I'd been before entering that forest.

I completed my magazine change, scanned for any additional enemies, and turned on my radio.

"Remy," I transmitted, my voice steel, "The sniper is dead."

Instead of his response I heard a deep, undulating thunder from the sky to my front, rolling slow and distant but growing louder as the seconds ticked by.

Remy's voice was panicked, feverish, like I'd never heard. "*They still can't make comms with the pilots! Apaches are inbound to smoke that hilltop!*"

The throbbing hum I now heard was the churning rotor blades of approaching attack helicopters. And I stood at the pinnacle of that forest, ground zero of their imminent attack.

But I didn't feel fear, or urgency; instead, a detached numbness overtook me as I replied, "Copy."

"*Copy?*" Remy spat back. Then, outraged, "*Copy?! Get the fuck out of there, Slick! Run, now!*"

I turned off my radio again.

I could have fled before Hellfire missiles impacted on top of me, their explosions preceding long bursts of 30mm chain gun. But instead I cast a final glance at my fallen enemy before proceeding toward the approaching helicopters.

The rotors grew louder as I stepped out of the forest, climbing atop a rocky crest to face the cobalt depths above me, feeling like I now stood at the top of the world. A rippling spine from a distant mountain range carved a line between sky and earth, the boundary spiky with pine trees.

Two distant dark specks were silhouetted against the endless blue expanse, growing in size and sound as they raced toward me. My lungs screamed for air, my mouth was parched with a cottony thirst as my adrenaline receded.

Yet I felt surreally calm as I reached back with one dirt-smeared hand, opened a pouch on my kit, and reached inside.

I pulled out a tightly rolled cloth and shook it free. My American flag unfurled to its full length, the red, white, and blue clear and vivid against the primitive landscape. I lifted my arms, letting the flag catch the wind so the Apaches could see it.

Now I could distinctly make out the angled profiles of the most advanced attack helicopters money could buy, their noses bulbous with advanced optics. Sunlight glinted against the panels of armored glass shielding the pilots, the insect-like extension of their chain guns rotating toward me.

Then the helicopters spun sideways on either side of the hilltop, exposing their armored bellies. Their stubby wings bore neatly aligned missiles and rocket pods while precision rotors carved a circular swath above them. Twin engines emitted streaky hazes of exhaust that blurred the air as they roared past, their sculpted tails vanishing in my periphery as I stood alone, tightly grasping my flag.

The distant horizon appeared bleak in the Afghan sun, obscured by desolate, barren trees silhouetted against the backdrop of endless mountains.

It was the first anniversary of 9/11. I'd just achieved the pinnacle of all I'd ever aspired to do: avenging my countrymen, defending my friends, and succeeding on the Ranger objective. In my first gunfight I'd demonstrated a rush of extraordinary audacity, and acted boldly, almost suicidally. And I'd done so for no clearly appointed end. But as I would soon discover, that spontaneous action would come to epitomize the subsequent years of my life.

Because darkness was soon to fall.

After that deployment to Afghanistan, and after the invasion of Iraq several months later, the fallout from war would take hold of me.

Six years to the day after narrowly defeating that

enemy sniper on a hilltop in Afghanistan, I would no longer be a Ranger.

I would be a mercenary, an assassin in exile far from my homeland.

And a new war would just be beginning.

* * *

Check out the next in series, Greatest Enemy!
Continue reading for a sample.

Sign up for the Reader List and be the first to know about new releases and special offers from former Green Beret and USA Today bestselling author, Jason Kasper.

Join Jason Kasper's Reader List at Jason-Kasper.com

GREATEST ENEMY: AMERICAN MERCENARY #1

David Rivers is an Army Ranger—a combat veteran of the wars in Afghanistan and Iraq. He has almost completed his final year at West Point when his world is turned upside down by a sudden discharge from military service. Angry and confused, David soon hits rock bottom.

And that's when they appear.

Three mysterious men. Men who know David's dark secret—they know that he has murdered someone in cold blood.

And they want him to do it again.

Get your copy today at Jason-Kasper.com

Turn the page to read a sample

GREATEST ENEMY: CHAPTER 1

June 1, 2008
Park Ridge, Illinois

The house was silent, and I passed through its shadows like a ghost.

Moonlight filtered through the horizontal slats of the blinds, its dull glow mottled by the trees and casting hazy shadows over me. As I rounded the corner of the entryway, the only sound that could be heard above the rustle of my clothes and the whisper of my footsteps on the carpet was the low hum of a refrigerator, its surface reflecting the twin green clocks of a microwave and oven.

I pivoted around a corner, both hands maneuvering the .22 pistol that hovered just beneath my field of vision. A crimson light marked the corner of an idling flat screen on the wall, and beneath it the black, gaping maw of a fireplace. Moving past them, I stopped at the corner to see a hallway receding into blackness.

After releasing one gloved hand from the gun, I made a fist and rapped three times on the wall.

White light abruptly framed a door at the end of the

hall, and the rack of a shotgun slide echoed throughout the house. In an instant, the door swung open and flooded the hallway with glaring light. I stepped back into the shadows as the long barrel of a 12-gauge Mossberg appeared from the door frame.

As the man holding the shotgun emerged from the room and swung the barrel toward me, I shot him twice in the gut.

He stumbled backward as the quick barks of my .22 faded, his back striking the far wall as he slumped into a seated position. One hand clutched his stomach while the other maintained a tenuous grip on the shotgun.

I stepped into the light and said, "Hello, Peter. I'm David Rivers."

He squinted up at me, panting in disbelief as a glimmer of recognition crossed his eyes.

"How's Laila?" he asked.

"This is between us now. You started our first conversation, and now I'm starting our last."

He swung the shotgun barrel toward my face and pulled the trigger.

A hollow click sounded.

"That's odd," I said, sliding my pistol into my belt. I walked forward and took the shotgun from his hand, which slid down his lap and fell limply to the floor. Then I reached into my pocket for the shells and began slipping them into the loading port.

He assumed a fearful, obedient look of submission, his now-empty hand uniting with the other over his stomach as bright red blood streamed through his fingers.

"Don't," he whispered between ragged breaths. "I can pay you... call them... get the ambulance."

"The last time we spoke, you lectured me on revenge. Do you want to lecture me now?"

"I never saw you, man. Just go. Please."

I loaded the final shell and shook my head.

"I told you this would happen, Peter. And I know you've probably talked shit without consequence on a thousand other occasions. But you finally did it at the wrong time to the wrong fucking person. And now"—I racked the slide to load a shell into the chamber—"you're about to get smoked in the face with your own shotgun."

Balling his hands into nervous fists against his bleeding gut, he cringed as if expecting me to slap him. "Listen to me for one fucking second. Just hear me out—"

"I gave you the chance to kill yourself, but you didn't have the brains or the balls to do the honorable thing. Maybe your dad didn't teach you right, or maybe you were born a coward and it's in your blood. Either way, I'm giving you a chance to face the consequences of your actions like you've never had to do."

"I've got close to twenty grand in the bedroom safe; just take it and go. The code is 62-29-99."

My face slid into a grin. "Peter, you're not listening. Accept your fate. You asked for me, and now you've got me. And no one's going to avenge you, because I'm swallowing a gun in a few hours. This is how your life is going to end."

"I'm begging you, I shouldn't have treated Laila like that. I didn't mean to... I'm sorry, I'm so fucking sorry—"

"Try and have some dignity at your death. You only get one."

"I'll do anything, just please don't fucking do this."

I angled the shotgun barrel level with his face. "At least you didn't cry."

At this, he began weeping like Laila had on the night he called her.

"Goodbye, Peter," I said, firing the Mossberg with a deafening blast.

His head vanished in an explosion of blood and smoke. As his shoulders slumped to the side, I lowered the barrel and watched the eerie postmortem twitch of his shoulders.

Then I dropped the shotgun at my feet, turned, and walked out of the house.

* * *

The neon liquor store sign glowed in the darkness, its seedy glare the same in every state I'd ever visited. I accelerated toward it, the tires of my twelve-year-old Explorer rumbling over the uneven surface of the pavement, which was saturated with rain that had only stopped minutes ago. The rest of the storefronts along the empty street were dark, now visible only by the distant radiance of streetlights until my headlights swept over them as I passed.

I sped up as I neared the liquor store. It was moments away from closing for the night, which I had realized abruptly when I reached my hotel and found that the bottle I'd packed was nearly empty.

After pulling into the abandoned lot, I found a dark parking spot between streetlights and then killed the engine. Snatching my backpack from the passenger seat, I hastily unzipped the main compartment to reveal my laptop case, which bore the scars of half a decade of travel. I paused for a moment before reaching past the laptop, feeling around in the bag until my fingers touched a cool, textured grip.

I withdrew the Ruger revolver, a steel bulldog that weighed more than double the pistol I'd just used to wound Peter. Opening the cylinder, I checked that it was fully loaded with six rounds stamped .454 CASULL, each capable of killing any big game on the planet. Satisfied, I snapped the cylinder shut and carefully slid the Ruger into my waistband before pulling my shirttail over it.

I set the backpack on the passenger seat, then stepped into the warm, humid air and strode toward the entrance.

An elderly vagrant in a green military jacket limped toward me from the side of the store.

"Hey, son," he called, "you got any change? Hey, son!"

I walked past him and pushed open the door, stepping into the bright lights of the store's interior.

A male voice called to me from behind the register, "We close in five minutes."

Walking through the aisles, I scanned the shelves until I found the rows of glass bottles with reassuringly familiar labels. I passed the scotches and whiskeys, then came to a halt in front of the house selection of bourbon. My eyes drifted to the top shelf, and I sighed in relief as I stretched out my hand to grasp the neck of a single, large bottle.

I brought it to chest height and cradled the bottom with my other hand as I appraised the neatly printed letters spelling WOODFORD RESERVE.

I frowned when I saw that the otherwise flawless bottle was marred with a cheap, lopsided green sticker that said, CLOSING TIME WINE & SPIRITS: $62.99.

As I approached the register, the college-aged Indian man behind the counter watched me.

"You look like a man on a mission."

I set down the bottle in front of him. "Yeah. Didn't realize I was running out of bourbon until just now."

"Busy night?"

"Something like that."

"You need a mixer?"

"And consume all those empty calories? I'm trying to live forever."

He examined the sticker on the bottle and typed the price into his register. "$68.16," he said.

I looked up at the vertical American flag suspended from the ceiling behind him, the drooping ripples in its fabric accumulating wide semicircles of dust.

"$68.16," he repeated, sliding the bottle into a brown paper bag and setting it upright on the counter.

I counted out four bills from my wallet and handed them to him. "Keep the change."

"Thanks. Need your receipt?"

"No."

"Have a good one."

I compressed the bag around the neck of the bottle and said, "I most certainly will. You do the same."

When I stepped outside into the damp night air, a voice beside me yelled, "Hey!"

The old man who had asked me for change was still standing there, and his weathered, unshaven face fixed on mine even as his shoulders swayed with drunkenness.

"Don't you ignore me," he demanded, his eyes welling up with tears. "I'm a veteran, goddammit."

I stopped and faced him, glancing down at the faded patches on his jacket. "Where'd you serve at, Staff Sergeant?"

"I was in Dak To in '67, fighting for your country. That's Vietnam, son."

I tucked the bottle under one arm and reached for my wallet. I pulled out a stack of bills, folded them in half, and handed them to him.

"That's everything I've got, Sarge. Treat yourself to the good stuff."

Returning to my truck, I settled into the driver's seat

and slammed the door shut behind me. I opened the backpack and was sliding the bottle of bourbon alongside my laptop when I heard the sudden, piercing wail of police sirens.

I looked out the windshield at the empty parking lot and, beyond it, the orbiting flashes of red and blue lights reflecting off storefronts in the distance. I took a deep breath and released it, then reached under my shirt to pull out the Ruger.

Rotating the revolver upward between my chest and the steering wheel, I pressed the warm steel ring of the muzzle against the underside of my jaw. My right finger settled on the smooth curve of the trigger, and I whispered to myself:

"Three."

The headlights of the first police car pierced the night, and were followed immediately by a second one.

"Two."

I became lost in the sirens' howling wails as their volume increased to a roar.

"One."

The glare of the flashing lights grew in intensity, nearly blinding me as I squinted into the flickering red-and-blue nothingness.

"See ya."

My finger tensed on the trigger as the police cars roared past my vehicle, their sirens receding as they sped along the wet street.

I released what seemed like an endless exhale, then lowered the pistol to my lap and took a few measured breaths. I slipped the Ruger back into my waistband and pulled my shirt over it once more.

Starting my truck, I turned on the headlights and pulled forward, gliding the car through a long puddle before turning onto the street and driving away from the sound of police sirens that, by then, had faded almost entirely.

* * *

As I walked down the hotel hallway toward my room with the heavy backpack slung over my left shoulder, I felt an overwhelming rush of relief. I would be able to spend my final hours drinking and writing, the last two exquisite pleasures in my life.

Coming to a stop before room 629, I fished the key card out of my pocket and slid it into the slot above the handle. When the light flashed green, I pushed open the door and stepped inside the modest room.

As I let the door slam shut behind me, my eyes fell to the corner table backed by a rolling chair. There, I would compose my final passage, my magnum opus. It would crown a thousand fragmented pieces of writing that had accumulated on the laptop like cancer cells over the nights spent sitting alone in the darkness, looking deep inside myself and becoming increasingly sickened by what I found.

My eyes ticked downward, registering wet footprints on the patterned carpet. In that same instant, I heard a man's voice coming from my left.

"Get your hands up, shithead."

My stomach dropped.

I held my hands open at waist level and looked through the bathroom doorway to the end of an automatic pistol emerging from the shadows, its barrel extending into a suppressor that was aimed at my chest.

A second voice said, "All the way up, David. Do it, or you're dead."

I glanced up to see the end of another handgun suppressor leveled at my face, the man holding it tucked behind the edge of the wall in front of the bed.

My mind raced in disbelief. I took a final breath, and did the only thing I could.

Yanking on my shirtfront with one hand, I seized the rubber grips of the Ruger with the other. I'd drawn the pistol in a split second, and was just beginning to rotate the barrel upward when the first man tackled me into the wall with the force of a freight train.

The revolver tumbled from my grasp as his shoulders drove me to the floor. Before I could recover from the initial impact, the second man advanced on me and delivered a crushing overhead blow to the side of my face.

My vision blurred, my mouth filled with thick blood, and pain exploded in my skull. The first man rolled me onto my back, yanking my upper body off the ground by my collar. In a blindingly fast three-part motion, he bounced my head off the ground, against the wall, and off the ground again.

I involuntarily coughed up an explosion of blood before he rolled me back onto my stomach. One of the men stripped the backpack from my left arm while the other jerked my hands upward to the small of my back.

I winced and grunted, "mother*fucker*," into the carpet as my wrists were cinched together with a narrow plastic restraint. The man straddling my back roughly frisked me, removing the contents of my pockets. I heard the rustling of paper and sloshing of bourbon as the other man searched my bag.

With half of my face smashed into the floor and my voice slurred with the blood in my mouth, I said, "You know, for a second there I thought you were the police."

The man above me grasped the side of my neck,

applying his body weight to pin me down further into the carpet. The boots belonging to the second man stepped in front of my face, and as I tried to roll my eyes upward, the end of a pistol suppressor was pressed against my temple, forcing my head back to the floor.

One of the men responded with a curt voice spoken between angry breaths.

"It would be better for you if we were. Trust me on that. And we know you killed Peter McAlister."

"What makes you say that?"

"Because we watched you do it."

"No, you didn't."

"We watched you get the spare key from the brick in the front walkway. Then we stood over him at the end of the hallway before his brains had dried on the wall. Is that specific enough for you, David?"

"We're getting there."

"This is where you tell us who paid you to kill him."

"No, it isn't."

At this, the hand on the side of my neck rotated around my jugular and squeezed, cutting off my air. The man pulled me up by my throat, lifting my chest off the ground before spinning me sideways. My shoulders slammed against the wall as I came to rest in a slouched sitting position.

When I opened my mouth to hollowly gasp for air, he slid the pistol suppressor between my teeth, pushing it to the back of my throat before releasing the pressure on my jugular. I snorted desperate breaths through my nostrils as I caught my first full glimpse of my attacker. His chest was as wide as my shoulders, and his dark eyes blazed with fury behind the handgun. I tried to pull my face away from the pistol, but he grabbed the back of my head and forced the suppressor deeper into my mouth.

"Talk around the gun. Who paid you to kill him?"

"How am I supposed to spit in your face with a pistol in my mouth?" I mumbled.

I heard the chirp of a radio, followed by a tinny voice that said, *"Black, Red."*

Somewhere to my right, the second man responded, "Go for Black."

"You're going to love what I found in his truck. This guy is coming with us."

My mind raced through the contents of my vehicle, settling on the black ballistic nylon bag hidden under a tarp.

The man hovering over me leaned in and said, "This isn't finished," before pulling the pistol out of my mouth, raising it high to the side, and swinging it back down across my head. I flinched a split second before the metal cracked against my skull.

Then, my entire world went black.

GREATEST ENEMY: CHAPTER 2

Five Years Earlier
March 23, 2003
Al-Jawf Air Base, Saudi Arabia

The raging sun slipped under the horizon, the endless sky blushing to a blazing orange hue in the final minutes before darkness.

The sight could not have been more welcomed by the men who watched it.

From the first moment it became visible until it descended into the other side of the earth, the sun over Saudi Arabia turned the world around us into an oven. Its merciless rays were amplified by the featureless, hard-packed sand that extended flat as a pool table in all directions and out to the horizon.

By the time nightfall arrived, my company of Army Rangers had already been sitting in rows on the ground beside the dirt airstrip for hours, sweating in desert camouflage chemical suits. Our gas mask carriers were slung between our thighs, and on top of those folded kit bags contained vests loaded with ammunition, grenades, and canteens that were pinned across our waists by harness straps from our static line parachutes. Massive rucksacks were attached to our hips below shoebox-sized reserves, adding an additional hundred-pound anchor to our load.

The majority of us were nineteen-year-old privates, and our purpose at any given time was dictated by slightly older team and squad leaders. Although we were young, if the government wanted to parachute 154 Americans behind enemy lines to capture an airfield and begin ransacking their way across enemy territory until the commanding general said to stop, then Rangers were the force of choice.

Until I had proven myself in Afghanistan the previous summer, my daily routine consisted of being punched in the stomach, thrown into wall lockers in the squad area, kicked in the ribs as I did push-ups on command, and conducting the aptly named "electric chair," which involved squatting against the wall while holding a twenty-pound machine gun tripod with arms extended—within minutes the body began to shake uncontrollably, giving the appearance of being electrocuted.

That type of personal and professional development was completely independent of structured training that included road marches, shooting, practicing raids, and patrolling through the woods late into the night and oftentimes into the following day.

The collective result of those efforts culminated in the scene before me: a group of men completely desensitized to violence, charged with testosterone, and bored by weeks of living in tents on the remote Saudi airfield. We had spent the days of March 2003 waiting for the Iraq invasion, and now required only the arrival of our airplanes to enter our second war in as many years.

Remington was seated on the ground beside me, his lanky features and darting eyes beginning to vanish in the fading light.

Speaking in a barely intelligible strain of Alabamian, he said, "You better give them hell up at West Point, David. Represent Gun Six. Who's supposed to be on my gun team once you're gone?"

"We've got to make it through the invasion first, Remy. And I'm not reporting to West Point until June."

"How many times you applied to that place, anyway?"

"Just twice."

"Who ever thought of you a-going to college," he drawled. He paused to spit a stream of wintergreen tobacco juice onto the dirt. "What did Sarah say when she found out you got in?"

"It'll delay the wedding a bit. She wasn't thrilled."

"Four years ain't a bit, Slick."

"Five. I have a year of prep school first."

"You think she's gonna wait around for that? Lemme see that picture again."

He often made the same request, though he had met her in person numerous times. I reached into a shoulder pocket and pulled out the dog-eared photograph I had been carrying with me since Afghanistan.

I handed it to him. "We've been together since we were fifteen, and I look like a fucking male model. She'll wait."

He turned on the red lens headlamp that hung around his neck, and its glow illuminated the glossy image of a slim, brunette teenager who was holding a teddy bear and smiling coyly at the camera from her college dorm room.

Remington examined it closely. "I hope I find me a girl like that someday."

"You're the best motherfucker I've ever met." I

switched my tone to imitate a deep Southern accent. "You'll find her, Remy."

Handing the picture back, he said, "I don't talk like that."

He talked exactly like that. Even when objecting, he pronounced "that" with two syllables: *thay-att*.

The First Sergeant shouted, "PLANES!"

Remington killed his headlamp, and I stuffed the picture back in my shoulder pocket as the churning hum of turboprops grew in volume. An MC-130 Combat Talon appeared out of the darkness and touched down on the airstrip several hundred meters away, roaring past us as three identical transport planes landed in rapid succession. They slowed to a halt and began turning around, whipping stinging sand across our faces. Remington and I struggled to rise as airfield staff moved from man to man, helping us to our feet.

The walk toward the aircraft quickly became a feat of extreme endurance. The two hundred meters that stretched between us and the planes felt like as many miles. Burdened by the weight of that much gear strapped to that many inconvenient places, our every movement was accomplished only through very small, duck-waddle steps that left us in excruciating pain. Airfield staff came to our rescue, lifting up the weight of our rucks while we staggered forward and helping to shuttle exhausted Rangers to the birds for boarding.

My line of jumpers reached the third aircraft and shuffled onto a ramp beneath the tail, turning around and sitting as close to one another as possible while facing the dim sky beyond the plane. Once the last man was situated, the interior went dark for a moment before illuminating us in a surreal red glow brought on by the flight lamps. The metal ramp in front of us closed, inching away our view of the night desert. It was accompanied by a long, high-pitched squeal that ended when it locked into place, encapsulating us in the aircraft. The low vibration inside the cabin heightened as the plane began taxiing to the runway, and then quieted once again as we slowed to a halt while waiting for takeoff.

Suddenly, the engines' hum increased to a fever pitch as they revved to full power, and our plane jolted and lurched forward down the runway. Our stomachs sank as the aircraft lifted off the ground and lined up with the other MC-130s banking north toward Iraq. The formation descended to avoid radar detection, and we began our flight two hundred feet above the desert.

Almost as soon as we crossed the border into Iraq, we began receiving enemy fire. The small windows over our heads glowed with the lightning flash of anti-aircraft tracers as our pilots dropped flares.

Two jumpmasters, posted at the jump door on either side of the aircraft, stood and yelled over the drone of the engines, "*TWENTY... MINUTES.*"

"Twenty minutes," the jumpers echoed.

One of the jumpmasters then yelled, "The Ranger Creed!"

Everyone in the cabin recited the familiar words in as much unison as the propeller noise would allow.

"*Recognizing that I volunteered as a Ranger, fully knowing the hazards of my chosen profession...*"

I basked in the anticipation of the mission to come, my thoughts drifting back to the crushing monotony of my life before the Army.

"*I accept the fact that as a Ranger, my country expects me to move further, faster, and fight harder than any other soldier...*"

During a history class on ancient Greece at the start of

my freshman year of high school, the teacher asked who among us would want to grow up in Athens, and who in Sparta. I was the only one who raised a hand for Sparta. When my teacher asked why, I said, "Because they win." The rest of the class stared at me with a mixture of disinterest and disgust, except for a girl named Sarah.

"Energetically will I meet the enemies of my country. I shall defeat them on the field of battle for I am better trained and will fight with all my might..."

I spent the rest of high school sitting in the back of the class and reading paperbacks about special operations from Vietnam to Somalia. My best friend and I often skipped school for a week at a time to go hiking in the Smoky Mountains, and I counted down the days until I could join the Army. Within a week of graduation, I kissed Sarah goodbye and left for basic training.

"Surrender is not a Ranger word. I will never leave a fallen comrade to fall into the hands of the enemy..."

Near the end of infantry training, we emerged from our tents one morning to find our drill sergeants still inside the cadre building. We milled outside for an hour before a lone drill sergeant opened the door and asked, "Who has family in New York City?" A handful of privates raised their hands. "Do any of you have family members who work in the World Trade Center?" All hands went down except one. "Come with me," the drill sergeant said.

"Readily will I display the intestinal fortitude required to fight on to the Ranger objective and complete the mission, though I be the lone survivor."

I was now in my element, working with like-minded people who chose to go into harm's way. In Afghanistan, I discovered that I was good in a gunfight. I didn't get scared. Sudden enemy fire, raids into desolate compounds, long patrols through mountainous valleys—

all of it had given me a laser-like focus that could last for hours. The first time Remy and I were almost killed by a Taliban rocket soaring a few feet over our heads and exploding nearby, we had laughed like children even as the blast's concussion knocked the wind from our lungs.

"*RANGERS LEAD THE WAY!*"

Beside their respective doors, the jumpmasters gave a final nod to one another before squaring off to face the jumpers. My thoughts returned to more immediate concerns. Once I had been rigged with parachute equipment, urination became impossible.

That was now over four hours ago.

"*TEN... MINUTES.*" In anticipation of the next command, we unclipped the safety line from the aircraft floor and stuffed the webbing and carabiner into an accessible pocket.

"*GET... READY.*"

A pause.

"*ALL PERSONNEL... STAND... UP.*"

Commotion ensued as we struggled to our feet to begin the ten excruciating minutes of standing before the lights beside each jump door would change from red to green.

"*HOOK... UP.*"

We unclipped the static line hook from our reserve parachute's carrying strap and snapped it onto the steel cable stretched over our heads.

"*CHECK... STATIC... LINES.*"

After inspecting the yellow length of my static line for tears from the hook-up point to where it disappeared over my shoulder, I proceeded to check Remington's line. The webbing snaked a predetermined distance back and forth behind his chute, which would automatically deploy once stretched taut as he dropped from the plane. Finding no issues, I tapped him on the helmet to let him know he was good.

"*CHECK... EQUIPMENT.*"

I ran my hand around my chin strap to ensure that I would not lose my helmet on exit, snapped my leg and chest straps to check that they were connected, and felt the lace holding the top of the weapon case on my side. My bladder felt like it was going to explode.

"*SOUND OFF FOR EQUIPMENT CHECK.*"

The signal started at the rear of the plane and passed like dominoes via a slap on the body and the word, "OKAY." I listened to Rangers yelling in succession from rear to front until I felt a hand smack my ribs, which I then relayed to Remington. The first jumper gave a final signal to the jumpmaster, who turned and slid his jump door upward and open. As the plane filled with the deafening roar of wind and turboprops, clouds of pale sand rolled inside. Rangers cheered as the jumpmasters began checking the jump doors. The familiar pain of standing uncomfortably with my parachute and full equipment began to grow.

"I have to pee so fucking bad," Remington shouted over his shoulder as we stood under the crushing weight of our gear.

"Me too."

The jumpmasters yelled something.

Remington asked, "Did they just say one minute?"

"I think so."

"*THIRTY... SECONDS.*"

"See you on the ground, Remy."

"Have a good jump, Slick."

I never saw the green light turn on or heard the command to "GO." Instead, the line of jumpers on the opposite side of the plane surged forward a moment before my row headed for the door. We shuffled forward, the noise of the engines and the shriek of the wind growing louder with each step. Deep, rhythmic whooshing noises accompanied each jumper's exit. Remington vanished out of the porthole and into the darkness. I handed my line to the safety, turned right to face the howl of the open door, and jumped into the black sky over Iraq.

* * *

Continue reading Greatest Enemy (American Mercenary #1): Get your copy today at Jason-Kasper.com

ALSO BY JASON KASPER

American Mercenary Series

Greatest Enemy
Offer of Revenge
Dark Redemption
Vengeance Calling
The Suicide Cartel
Terminal Objective

Shadow Strike Series

The Enemies of My Country

Spider Heist Thrillers

The Spider Heist
The Sky Thieves
The Manhattan Job

Standalone Thriller

Her Dark Silence

Want to stay in the loop?

Sign up to be the FIRST to learn about new releases. Plus get newsletter only bonus content for FREE.

As a thank you for signing up, you'll receive a free copy of *The Ranger Objective*. Join today at **Jason-Kasper.com/newsletter**

ACKNOWLEDGMENTS

Thanks to the team that made this story possible!

As always, my sister and content editor Julie revised my rough draft to a decipherable state.

My team of pre-beta readers then weighed in to guide my rewrites: Codename: Duchess, Derek, John "JB" Presley, and JT.

The following beta readers provided their feedback and guided my hand in polishing this manuscript:

Bill Dunlop (USA Retired, 30 years service), Chet Manly, Earl Kelley, Howard, Gabi Rosetti, Jon Suttle, Jeane Jackson, M Julien, Mike Rajkowski (an old friend), Randy, Jack Raburn (Sierra Fox Alpha), Jim (B737), and Ray Dennis.

At this point in my writing career, I know better than to proceed without my editor! The unrivaled Cara Quinlan treated this short story prequel with the same care and attention to detail as a full-length novel, and for that I'll be forever grateful.

Finally, my beautiful and long-suffering wife Amy once again read, reviewed, and supported the production of this story, just as she has my entire portfolio.

ABOUT THE AUTHOR

Jason Kasper is the USA Today bestselling author of the Spider Heist, American Mercenary, and Shadow Strike thriller series. Before his writing career he served in the US Army, beginning as a Ranger private and ending as a Green Beret captain. Jason is a West Point graduate and a veteran of the Afghanistan and Iraq wars, and was an avid ultramarathon runner, skydiver, and BASE jumper, all of which inspire his fiction.

Never miss a new release! Sign up for the Reader List at Jason-Kasper.com/newsletter

Join the Facebook Reader Group for the latest updates: facebook.com/groups/JasonKasper

Contact info:
Jason-Kasper.com
Jason@Jason-Kasper.com

twitter.com/kasperauthor
instagram.com/kasperauthor

Made in the USA
Coppell, TX
17 September 2022